HURI

ldress

ALSO BY AMIT CHAUD

A Strange and Sublime Ad

Afternoon Raag

Freedom Song

A New World